LOVE IN THE SECURITY DIRECTORATE

A SECURITY DIRECTORATE SHORT STORY

ALEXANDRIA BLAELOCK

Also by Alexandria Blaelock

SHORT STORY COLLECTIONS
The Histories of Hayward Hall
Lovelorn, Lovestruck and Love at First Sight
Common or Garden Variety Heroes
Case Files of the Wilkinson Detective Agency
Unavoidable Fates
Christmas Travesties
Five Faces of Felicia Clarke
Little Place Called Home

FICTION
That Love Nonsense
Taipan vs Brown
The Ghost and Ms Cox
Friends Like That

MS BLAELOCK'S BOOKS
Stress Free Dinner Parties
Signature Wardrobe Planning
Holistic Personal Finance
Minimally Viable Housekeeping
Planning a Life Worth Living

A SELECTION OF AVAILABLE SHORT STORIES
Alma's Grace
Fate in Your Hands
Lady of the Looking Glass
Morning Star, Evening Star, Superstar
Secret Singer
Shining Star
Ship in a Bottle
Simone Says Hands in the Air
The Day the Schedule Broke

LOVE IN THE SECURITY DIRECTORATE

A SECURITY DIRECTORATE SHORT STORY

ALEXANDRIA BLAELOCK

BlueMere Books
MELBOURNE, AUSTRALIA

For permission requests, please contact
enquiries@bluemerebooks.com.

Ordering Information:
Discounts are available on quantity purchases. For details, contact orders@bluemerebooks.com.

Love in the Security Directorate/Alexandria Blaelock
paperback ISBN: 978-1-925749-20-5
digital ISBN: 978-1-925749-21-2

Book Layout © BookDesignTemplates.com
Cover Art © Tithi Luadthong/Depositphotos

LOVE IN THE SECURITY DIRECORATE

Captain Seraphina Robinson forced herself to take a power stance; spine straight, feet slightly spread, hands lightly clasped behind her back as she coolly observed her "husband" to be.

She knew of Major Callan Muir, of course, they'd met at the University of Civilisation.

Technically, the University was open to all citizens.

But everyone knew it was only for those who survived the State Academy of Cultural Regulation and were destined for higher positions than the Protection Squadron.

And to get into the Academy, you needed a Genomics Bureau classification proving you had a certain kind of genetic ability. The kind known colloquially as a "superpower."

Ideally achieved through the Directorate eugenics programme.

She'd admired his quiet stillness and was fascinated by his deep, resonant, and commanding voice. Perhaps that was his "superpower", though you never spoke of those.

He was very popular, always the centre of a group of sycophantic women.

Rumour had it he'd ended more than one promising career with unsanctioned intimate relationships.

She knew her career would end soon enough, but she'd wanted to make the best of it while she could.

He was only an inch or two taller than her, yet he and his fresh citrus cologne seemed to take up too much space in the tiny office they stood in.

His sleek dark hair, precisely cut to regulation length and style, was slightly crimped by the peaked cap now lightly gripped between his body and arm.

He was fortunate; his black officer's dress uniform perfectly suited his head and body shape.

And his medals took up an impressive amount of space across his broad chest.

She enjoyed a quiet moment of gratitude that her husband was attractive.

And around her age.

Unlike poor Asrani; paired with a fat, ugly man twice her age. Though they seemed to get on well enough.

And according to Asrani, he was faithful to her too.

It was too soon to tell what kind of husband the Major would be.

History suggested not faithful, but you didn't gain rapid advancement by taking stupid risks.

Maybe it was just a matter of the time you needed to get to know your partner.

She took a deep breath and resisted the urge to touch the smooth, unblemished skin of his face.

Scratching her palm instead.

He didn't seem to have aged a day.

Major Muir turned smartly as the Registrar pushed the door open, and entered with a large, red leather-bound ledger.

He sat at the desk and opened the book.

"The Genomics Bureau has paired you, Major Callan Muir, with you, Captain Seraphina Robinson, in an exclusive and binding five-year contract.

"You will now live together until the Bureau sees fit to terminate the contract between you.

"Do you declare before me that you come here voluntarily, and are without reservation prepared to do as the Bureau requires?"

"I do," they replied simultaneously.

"Major Muir," the Registrar said, "repeat after me; I, Major Callan Muir, take Captain Seraphina

Robinson as my allocated spouse to love, respect and care for."

Without hesitation, he did. And then it was her turn.

"I, Captain Seraphina Robinson, take Major Callan Muir as my allocated spouse to love, respect, and care for."

"Well done," the Registrar said. "I know you had little notice, but were you able to get rings?"

Callan pulled a fancifully engraved silver coloured band from his pocket.

"Major Muir, please place your ring on Captain Robinson's finger as a symbol of your commitment to her, and submission to the will of the State."

His hands were comfortingly warm against her cold ones. Firm and soft as he took her left hand and placed the ring, warm from his pocket, on her finger.

"Captain Robinson?" the Registrar asked.

She fidgeted. "I was recalled from my mission this morning to be notified of the union, so I don't have a ring."

"Not to worry," said the Registrar, pulling open a drawer in the desk, "you may use this band until you get an appropriate replacement.

"Captain Robinson, please place the ring on Major Muir's finger as a symbol of your commitment to him, and submission to the will of the State."

She took the cold and heavy ring from the Registrar and slipped it on Callan's finger.

"Excellent." The Registrar offered Callan a pen, "if you'd sign the register please."

Callan signed with a neat, compact signature and handed the pen to her. She signed her name and gave the pen back to the Registrar.

"Congratulations on your union. You may kiss."

They exchanged the required cheek kisses, right, left, right, and that was it.

They were "married," as the normals called it. At least for the time being.

"Your belongings are being transferred to your new quarters," he scribbled on a paper and passed it to Callan.

"Here's the address. May your union be long and fruitful."

They inclined their heads respectfully to the Registrar. Callan replaced his cap, turned to her, and offered his ring-clad hand.

She pursed her lips slightly, but took it.

As they left the room, she took a deep breath of unscented air, though it didn't dissipate the strength of his presence of the heat of his hand.

They walked down the corridor to the lift well, where she pushed the down button.

Now she was married to someone she barely knew.

The match probably had very little to do with them, and more to do with the offspring they might produce.

While she was mildly curious about what they hoped the children would be, it didn't really matter.

If they passed the Genomics Bureau's post-natal testing, they'd go to the Academy as she had, and it was unlikely she'd see them again.

And if they didn't, well, it was unlikely she'd see them again.

She glanced up at Callan, to see his full lips smiling slightly, and quickly looked away. Her heart skipped a beat, and she swallowed nervously.

What did you say to someone you barely knew but had entered a State-sanctioned relationship with?

It wasn't as if the children couldn't be created in a lab, so it was more likely they were supposed to monitor each other.

After all their training, was it even possible they'd be able to trust each other enough to love, respect, and care for each other?

Hopefully.

Seraphina wanted someone to love, respect, and care for her, but did he?

More importantly, *would* he?

Mind you, if there were no children, it probably wouldn't be a long union, so it wouldn't matter anyway.

He gave her hand a light squeeze. "It's an odd situation, isn't it?"

Her smile was more of a grimace as she turned to look at him again.

Partnered or not, it was unseemly to touch in public. She pulled her hand, but he didn't release it.

"I didn't expect to be paired so soon after graduation."

"It's not really that soon. It's been five years."

"I know, but I didn't imagine I'd be called back mid-assignment for this."

She sighed, "I've important work to complete, and it'll be months before I'm permitted to return."

"I agree marriage doesn't seem as important as some other matters, Captain Robinson, but perhaps you'll find it easier if you think of it as a new assignment with different objectives."

She looked at him sharply, but he seemed serious.

And, perhaps it was good advice - was that the key to a long and fruitful union?

She licked her lips.

At some point, the fruitful part had to be a factor.

The lift arrived, and the occupants looked curiously at them as they shuffled around to make room. It wasn't often you saw people touching in public, let alone with bare skin. Callan entered, pulling her in behind him.

«« • »»

Callan was so happy.

He'd known from the moment he first saw her at University, that she was the one he wanted to spend his life with.

Her fitted uniform emphasised her curves in the best possible way, and the seams of her stockings were as straight as her spine.

She'd smoothed her fiery red hair into the regulation chignon, though a lock had fallen loose and curled seductively down her straight back.

Then she'd turned around, and they'd locked eyes for a moment before someone stole her attention away. But it was enough.

She'd glowed, literally glowed, like a bright golden beacon on the edge of the dark group she was with.

He'd tried to get closer as their years at University progressed, but somehow she always slipped away at the last minute.

She glowed when she saw him, and he didn't see her glowing at anyone else.

He wanted to know more.

Not that unauthorised relationships were permitted, and she was clearly the kind of person who followed the rules.

So, he formed a plan and learned what he could from the women who'd made themselves available to him.

And how the time had finally come, and he was ready for her.

It had taken almost the entire intervening period to prove himself and his precognitive abilities.

He'd progressed quickly up the ranks so that when he said Seraphina was to be allocated to him, no one doubted it was true.

And even though he hadn't in truth seen any such thing, when he saw her glow burst out as he'd entered the Registrar's office, all his doubts were laid to rest.

Even her light floral fragrance had reached out towards him.

He wondered if her power involved light and clarity, but you never talked about that.

Least of all, in enclosed spaces where it was highly likely you were being monitored.

Like their new home probably would be.

Still holding hands, they exited the lift.

She'd stopped trying to free herself the minute he'd pulled her into the lift, and when they reached the coat check, he was reluctant to let her go.

Though now they were paired, there was nowhere else she could go.

He held out her greatcoat so she could easily slip her arms into the sleeves, and lingered perhaps a moment too long as he smoothed it across her shoulders.

She was his to do as he wanted to, but he wanted her to love, respect, and care for him.

As he already did for her.

He shrugged into his own greatcoat, imagining how sweet the future would be in a union of affection, not just duty.

As they left the building, he took her hand and tucked it through his arm before putting his hand in his pocket.

The contours of her body fit neatly against his own. "It's a beautiful day, and it's not far to our new home. Shall we walk?"

She shrugged, and her whole body moved against him, a chaste preview of the passion he hoped was to come.

There was no rush. They granted newly partnered Directorate officers several weeks' leave, as a matter of course, so he set a leisurely pace.

It seemed the sun lit up the street ahead of them, though he hoped it was her.

"How have you been since University Major Muir?"

"Well, that feels a little awkward now we're partnered, doesn't it? Please call me Callan."

She nodded once, "of course Callan. You may call me Sera."

"Thank you, Sera. Obviously, I can't tell you about the classified work I've been doing, but I've been well. How about you?"

"About the same Callan," her cheeks coloured slightly, "I was excited to have the opportunity to travel with my work. Did you?"

"No, I've been based here in the City. Now and again, I get a leave pass and take a day trip to the countryside. Perhaps I can visit you when you return to your post?"

"I expect that would be acceptable."

He winced, but she probably hadn't spent the intervening period obsessively following his career the way he had hers.

Somehow, she'd fallen into step with him, so that was a hopeful sign.

And she'd left her hand where he'd put it, so he risked covering it with his own. "Have you spent much time in the City then?"

"Only periodic visits for planning sessions and further training. I don't think it's changed much since University."

"Here and there." He knew she'd studied Ancient History at University, and thought he could tempt her.

"They opened the New Ancient History Museum last year. We could visit it together if you like?"

She looked up at him, "I'm not sure it would be your thing, but yes, I'd like that."

He smiled down at her and inwardly pumped his fist into the air.

A brave street urchin approached the Protection Squadron officers. "Five dollars for a rose for the lady sir?"

The blossom was probably stolen, but he bought a red one anyway and leaning across, held it to her nose to smell.

Its sweet perfume seemed to pull them closer together.

He looked at her lips, and she licked them, then blushed daintily.

He pinned the rose to the collar of her coat, then tucked her hand back into the crook of his arm.

All too soon they were standing on the footpath outside the ugly yet compelling Brutalist-style building housing their new apartment.

The sun slanting through the clouds gave it a golden halo as they looked up at its stark horizontal lines.

Her jaw dropped a little. "It's beautiful, but surely there's some kind of mistake. This is much too lavish."

"Well, I am a Major, and we do have a position to maintain."

It wasn't too far from the truth, but he'd called in a few favours to have one of the smaller apartments allocated to them as a residence.

And they should be able to make some favourable connections from this base. "Let's go in and see what it's like."

He opened the door for her, allowing her to enter first.

But now it was his home, even he was a little over-awed by the brightly lit, highly polished concrete foyer.

A uniformed concierge with a small sidearm approached. "Major Muir, Captain Robinson?" They nodded in reply.

"This way please, you're in apartment 1202." He escorted them to the lift and pushed the call button. "Your things have been unpacked, and the apartment made ready for your arrival."

When the lift arrived, he gestured for them to enter the brass lined capsule before following and pressing the button for the twelfth floor.

«« • »»

Sera stepped a little closer to Callan and slipped her hand into his.

The building was imposing, and it was clearly luxurious living accommodation for high-ranking officers.

She was a little afraid they'd be asked to leave before they reached their new home.

When the lift reached their floor without incident, the concierge gestured to the left, and they obediently started walking in that direction.

The apartment was only three down from the lift well, so before long, he was opening the door to let them in. "Welcome to your new home."

He handed Callan the key. "If you need anything, dial 9 for the front desk, and we'll arrange it for you."

Callan thanked him and slipped something into his hand before he turned and walked away.

They were left standing at the open door, hand in hand, looking down a brightly lit corridor into their new home.

"I'm a little nervous," she said.

He smiled, "me too, but maybe this will help."

He pulled her into his arms, and kissed her on the lips, before pulling back to look at her.

Taken by surprise, her crush rekindled, she reassured herself this was now a sanctioned relationship.

She'd nothing to lose, just his love, respect, and care to gain.

Sera cupped his smooth cheek in her hand and looked up into his eyes for a long moment before kissing him back.

Callan groaned and crushed her body to his, before sweeping her off her feet and carrying her over the threshold.

«« • »»

The funny thing was, while he'd visited other apartments in this building, he had no idea where the bedroom was in this one.

So he walked down the corridor to its end, where he gasped at the view of the sun setting over the City.

She slipped from his arms and walked towards the glass sliding doors separating them from the balcony, taking off her coat and throwing it on a nearby comfy chair.

The view of her back was as enticing as the first time he'd seen it. Her movements were smooth and elegant as she removed her hat and jacket and threw them after the coat.

He struggled out of his coat, then stepped forward and wrapped his arms around her, leaning his chin on her shoulder to share the view.

She jumped, but leaned her head against his, "I've never seen anything as beautiful as this, have you?"

"No. It's breathtaking."

"I can't believe this is our new home. I thought it'd be a poky flat in the Shambles."

He smiled and kissed her neck, "I didn't think it would be that bad, but I think we can assume that the quality of our work has been rewarded with this residence."

She smiled and rubbed her face against his cheek. "I might be wrong, but I think I noticed a bottle of wine as you barged through the door."

He reluctantly let her go and backed away.

As he turned towards the room, he took off his cap and threw it on a chair, before sending his jacket and tie to follow.

His medals clinked gently as they landed.

He saw the wine chilling in an ice bucket with two glasses on the dining table as he was rolling up his sleeves.

He poured the wine and brought it back to her, now leaning on the balcony handrail, glowing brighter than the dying sunlight.

"Here's to you, and a long and happy life together."

She blushed again, took the glass and clinked it against his. "No, here's to you."

He sat on a slatted wooden seat and patted the space next to him. Sera looked at him for a moment, then kicked off her shoes and sat, curling up into his armpit.

He grunted as a hairpin dug into his underarm.

Putting his wine down, he started undoing her hair, gently pulling out a pin at a time.

Her breath quickened as he ran his fingers through it, drinking in its perfume until it was a river of fire down her back.

Pushing the weight of it aside, he kissed the nape of her neck and was rewarded when she turned to kiss him.

He thought he'd take it slow. They barely knew each other, and they had a long union ahead of them.

But then she slipped a hand between the buttons on his shirt.

Her fingers were still cool from the wineglass, and when they touched his hot skin, he knew he couldn't wait.

Taking her by the hand, he led her back into the apartment, throwing open door after door until he found the bedroom.

THE END

ABOUT THE AUTHOR

Alexandria Blaelock writes stories, some of them for *Ellery Queen's Mystery Magazine* and *Pulphouse Fiction Magazine*.

She's also written five selfhelp books applying business techniques to personal matters like getting dressed, cleaning house, and feeding your friends.

She lives in a forest because she enjoys birdsong, and the smell of gum leaves. When not telecommuting to parallel universes from her Melbourne based imagination, she watches K-dramas, talks to animals, and drinks Campari. At the same time.
Discover more at www.alexandriablaelock.com.

IF YOU ENJOYED THIS STORY...

try the other Security Directorate stories

... or the collections

Why not try The Ghost and Ms Cox

Life interrupted

To say the letter was a surprise was an understatement. It arrived addressed to Miss Finlay Cox, which made the contents even more extraordinary.

Orphan Finn Cox inherits a cottage. Thinks it holds the key to her origins. Of course she takes a look. Who wouldn't?

But when she gets there, she gets more than she bargained for.

Is it friend, family or foe?